THE CITY ON THE OTHER SIDE

THE CITY
ON THE
OTHER SIDE

MAIRGHREAD SCOTT

ROBIN ROBINSON

First Second
NEW YORK

Once upon a time, there was a kingdom of fairies called the *Seelie*.

Bright and shining, these fairies touched every aspect of our world.

They blessed fern and bird and human beings alike.

But there was another kingdom of fairies. One whose job it was to bless worm and stone and crumbling log.

They were called the *Unseelie*.

Many conflicts arose between them. But even though they had been at peace for centuries, these two kingdoms...

...were, again, at war.

--it is not about dishonor, my lord. It--

King Ro'hish!

Our walls are breached. Unseelie are inside the castle!

You must go now, my lord!

This is one of the last Seelie forts in this area. If we lose it **and** you, the war is over.

Your concern touches my heart, dear friends.

But much of my power has already passed to my daughter. *She* is the key to defeating Coscar. Not I.

There is no word from Id'naress, Your Highness.

We can't even be sure she's alive.

Oh, Coscar.

You ask for the one thing you will never have.

"The necklace is already gone."

And you will never see it again until you release my daughter from wherever you imprisoned her!

Lies! Your daughter abandoned her--

She tried to destroy the Unseelie. I stopped her. She ran. Don't blame me for this war, blame *her*.

Besides, you're only upset that we destroyed you first.

KRCK

Id'naress is not some innocent prisoner. She is in hiding, pretending to be a martyr even as she protects her own skin.

Spine! Gather my scouts and find the necklace. It can't be far.

10

But the fairy world is not the only world. The human world continued...

...unaware of the war that was destroying them as well.

Quickly, ladies. Madam is already at table.

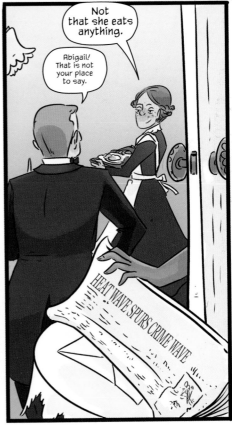

Not that she eats anything.

Abigail! That is not your place to say.

HEAT WAVE SPURS CRIME WAVE

Isabel!

Mother?

A woman of breeding is never late to breakfast.

Especially not on her mother's last day before her trip. I'll be relieved to have some distance between me and this filthy city.

I like the city.

Nonsense! Europe is the place to see, and I will take you along with me someday.

I don't want to see Europe; I want to see the city here.

You see it all the time, when Charles takes you to your tutors.

I don't let you wander through the rubble and I won't apologize for wanting my daughter clean and well-cared for.

It'll be good for you to visit your father this summer.

Why doesn't he ever visit us?

Your father is a very busy man.

Your father is quite the sculptor, miss. I'm sure you'll learn a great deal from him.

And you haven't been to Carmel in so long it's practically a new place. How exciting!

Mother doesn't like me to get dirty. I remember there being lots of dirt in the country, right?

Perhaps. But you never know what's around a corner until you take the turn.

Thank you, Charles.

All part of the job, miss.

19

21

*Princesa!** How is my little girl?

Hello... Father. How are you?

Please! It's Papa! So formal, this one.

*Princess

And Papa... is under a very tight deadline with his latest sculpture.

But, of course, an independent little girl like you can amuse yourself while I work.

I suppose.

Give my love to Rosalia, Charles. We'll handle things from here.

Good-bye, Charles.

Your room is *mostly* set up. It just needs a little elbow grease.

What do you think?

Not as spotless as your *mother* would want, but we don't have to tell her, do we?

No, Papa.

Fear not, princesa. I'll be back as soon as I finish one last step. Minutes only, I promise.

You don't need to lift a finger.

26

Nonono!

Rarrr

Shoo. You can't eat flowers.

Oh, no! I'm sorry! I didn't mean to get...

...dirty.

Hmm.

Charles said get the pan hot first, then--

errh...

Princesa!

What are you doing? I said I'd be right back.

I was just making eggs.

That is for Papa to do.

Here. We can't have a princesa getting burnt fingers on her first day here, can we?

No, Papa.

See, princesa? Papa has everything under control.

But, he does need his princesa's help with one thing.

Papa must get back to work and he needs you to be a big girl and put yourself to bed.

But it's not even dark yet.

KRCH! SHHK SHHHK

Papa?

How...how do you see me? Why am I on this side of the Veil?

I don't-- Are you okay?

No. The Unseelie... They are coming.

I'm sorry. I don't know what that means.

Are you hurt--?

What's happening? I can't move my hand!

It's the necklace. I--I'm not sure what's going on.

Isabel...It means "God is my oath." I need you to make an oath to me now, Isabel.

Yes. Anything.

Do not be so eager. It is unfair of me to ask it at all.

But the necklace responds to you. It must mean something...

This necklace must go to the Seelie general, Miyori.

No! Please stay awake.

He is in the city, but I know not... where.

He must have it. Everything... Everything depends on it.

Swear... that... you...

I promise.

...I just...don't know who Miyori is.

Pfft! Well, stick close to Ol' Button, kiddo.

Ol' Button? More like Old Loudmouth.

You just jumped into the deep end, feet first.

Wait! We're helping? Why are we helping? I don't think we should get involved.

hehehehe

We're just telling her what's going on.

But what if...Coscar... finds out we helped?

Who's Coscar?

One nasty guy, spriteling.

An antlered, grasping, know-nothing monolith. That's what he is.

"There are two types of fairies in our kingdom, the Seelie and the Unseelie."

"Unlike human kingdoms, fairies switch who's in control. Each court has a monarch who rules for half the year."

"For us, that's Id'naress and Coscar."

"Now, each court is supposedly equal. But *we're* all Seelie here."

"And Unseelie are pointy, slimy, and don't play well with others...especially not humans."

"This isn't the first Cold Iron War."

"That's what it's called when fairy fights fairy."

"But it could be the last."

"Coscar decided he didn't want to share power with humans, or the Seelie, or anybody else."

"He kidnapped Id'naress, hid her away, and stole her power."

"Coscar declared himself to be king and the Unseelie to be in charge forever.

"King Ro'hish is fighting, but he gave up most of his power to Id'naress, and Coscar's been more powerful than anyone expected.

"The city's completely under Coscar's control. Everyone lives by his laws.

"And every day he takes more of the forest as well."

"How long has Id'naress been missing?"

"Don't you remember it?

"It was the day your city burned."

Coscar caused the earthquake? But that was in my world!

Our worlds aren't separate, spriteling.

There's barely a grass blade's width of magic between them.

We call it the Veil.

But just because it separates us doesn't mean we don't affect each other.

A war on our side makes the earth jiggle like jelly on your side. A building built on your side gives us itchy roots.

So if Coscar wins, the city could be destroyed all over again!

Possibly. Coscar doesn't like humans. If he gains complete control over our realm, he may wage war on yours next.

All the more reason to grab our spores and go!

A Seelie messenger puffed out her last breath to say knobby knees here has gotta get this necklace to the city, and I intend to make sure she does it! Who's with me?!

...I don't know how we can help.

Help?! I lived in the city. I know it like the back of my hand.

I *served* in the army.

A reeeaaal long time ago.

I'd take the dang thing myself except...well, when a necklace does more than look pretty, I've found it's best to leave it be.

And since no one *else* is volunteering...

Miss, you just follow Button. I'll get you to where you need go.

But you don't have to. You're still very young. You don't need to go.

I...

46

47

At least not in **my** world.

I'm going to the city.

A-**HA!** What did I tell you? She's a true warrior! Practically a Seelie herself!

Onward!

Um...Mr. Button? Do we have time for me to pack a few things first?

Right! But make it quick; we have a couple of worlds to save.

Hurry up, Izzy. The sooner we bag that Unseelie menace the sooner you can get back to your dad.

Of course... when I come back.

Sooo tiiired...

Where is the necklace? The messenger?!

My lady, we killed the messenger but don't have the necklace.

What?! Coscar ordered the necklace be returned!

It wasn't our fault!

Pffft

There was a magic girl, a human. She drove us away and stole the necklace!

Humans aren't magic! That's the whole point of them!

She was! And she was on this side of the Veil! She used the necklace!

A human with magic? That can only be trouble.

What did she look like?

Uhhh... human?

Yes! Very human. Two eyes, a mouth, everything.

THEY ALL HAVE THOSE!

She was short...shorter than me. Her hair and skin were brown. And her petals were blue.

And you'd recognize her, if you saw her again?

Hey... You with me?

That quake hurt us, too, kiddo. No Seelie worth their skin'll let him do that again.

And with me on the case, Coscar's gonna be out of commission before he can even think about it.

With your help, of course.

After all, you've got longer legs.

We don't wanna miss our train.

Don't stare. You're already drawing people's notice as it is, looking so... human.

I mean, if you were purple it'd be something, but...

I *am* human.

I can't help what I look like.

Trust me, I know.

I think I recognize the store across the way. There was a store like it in *my* Carmel.

But even though it's in the same place, it's not here in the same way. Does that make sense?

As much sense as humans ever make. Stay here and sit tight. I'll scout out the train station.

GENERAL STOR

Unseelie jerks.

...Okay... huff...there's good news and bad news.

What's the good news?

Well, they haven't completely locked down the station and we're not currently in jail.

But the platform is swarming with Unseelie guards.

A human can't just walk past them. We'll be caught, tortured, and when they find out about the necklace it'll be over.

If a *human* walks past them.

Hey, you! Stop!

You don't want to lose your peaches. Right?

Sure wouldn't, sir.

Toldja.

Just take a seat and don't let that necklace do anything weird.

Now we just need to sit tight until we get there.

I thought humans can't be on this side of the Veil.

They can't.

Well, *he* can!

Stop!

Isabel! *Wait!*

Ouf!

Heh... Wrong door.

Ergh!!

That kid's run away from guards before!

What do you think you're doing?

If this is how he did it--

--it's how we'll do it, too.

Button...?

Well, at least the necklace is working for us!

foosh

Ah!!!

Why did you try to steal my necklace?

Stop followin' me! You're gonna get me arrested.

You tried to rob me! I'm not going to feel *bad* for you.

I steal to *live.* It's not like a lot of fairies are looking to adopt a *human* child.

Because humans are supposed to be on your side of the Veil.

She's here! Plus she's got weird powers. Yell at her!

I'm not "she," I'm Isabel and this is Button.

77

We're on a mission from the Seelie court!

Um, not that it's any of your business.

You're a Seelie agent? Ha! They must be desperate if they're recruiting little kids now.

'Cause you're so old?

I'm at least two years older than you and I've spent almost my whole life on this side 'a the Veil.

And do you have a name, Mr. Two-Years-Older?

It's Benjie.

Good, now we're introduced.

How did you get here anyway? Can you move from one side to the other all on your own?

It was the quake...

Not a lot of people made it out of Chinatown. No one seemed to want to save us. And I'm not even Chinese; I'm Filipino.

"When the quake hit, my parents put me in a closet. It was safer."

Help! *Please!* Someone!

Skritch
Skritch

Mom? Please...

"But I couldn't get out and no one could hear me.

"Except her."

Who...are you?

"Id'naress pulled me to her side of the Veil.

"She saved me.

"She said she'd come back for me.

"But she never did. They say she died, like my parents.

"Ever since then I've been able to move back and forth whenever I want."

I just didn't have anything to go back to.

How did you survive?

Stealing, mostly. Fairies are obsessed with stuff that humans don't think twice about.

And don't get high and mighty, fungus.

Losing a bit of ribbon doesn't ruin anyone's life, but it keeps mine going.

So, if Id'naress saved you...will you help us save her? We need to find someone named Miyori.

You don't want me.

I don't have anyone else.

...Fine.

Miyori's a Seelie general in the Unseelie capital, though. You'll never find him.

But someone has to know where he is. Fairies eat... Don't they?

Of course they do. Some a lot more than others. Right, fungus?

Okay, so Miyori needs supplies.

Anyone moving things on the black market needs Frogfoot's permission.

Frogfoot? Never heard of him.

He's a criminal! He's not exactly throwing himself a parade.

Frogfoot is the top boss of the entire city. If anyone knows where Miyori is, he does.

But if he keeps such a low profile, how do we find this Frogfoot exactly?

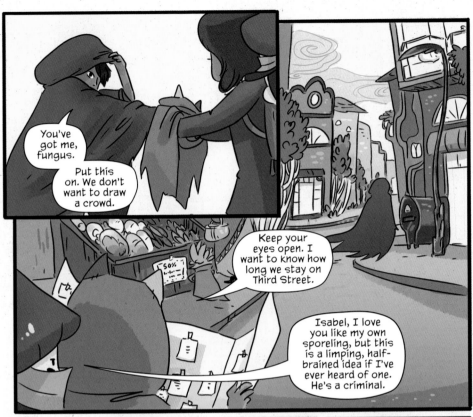

You've got me, fungus.

Put this on. We don't want to draw a crowd.

Keep your eyes open. I want to know how long we stay on Third Street.

Isabel, I love you like my own sporeling, but this is a limping, half-brained idea if I've ever heard of one. He's a criminal.

Id'naress trusted him.

I don't want to speak ill of the princess, but who knows what she saw in this short-panted huckster.

Follow *my* lead, Isabel. I'll keep you--

Shh!

Stick close, you two. Chinatown isn't always safe. Especially for weirdos like you.

Benjie, how do you know this Frogfoot person?

I told you, Frogfoot runs all the smuggling in the city. I have to sell to **someone**.

Is he Seelie?

Yeah, but he's still a smuggler and not the nicest person.

He's not terrible, I mean... Everything's just been so mixed up since the war started.

Just, don't say anything. Follow my lead and it'll all be fine.

Why is it always everyone else who's leading?

Do you enjoy the hunt, Torrent?

Actually... my race is vegetarian; we don't normally--

I mean, yes! I can't wait to **get** that human.

I'm shaking in my scales. The girl is the priority; she has the necklace, but I want **both** the humans if I can get them.

And the fairy they're traveling with.

Just follow my fin.

He'll want to see us. Trust me.

Ha! "Trust me," says the thief.

You trust thieves?

Try not to.

Well, I'm *not* a thief. I'm a *Seelie agent* and--

Isabel... quiet.

You will stand aside right now or I'll speak with your supervisor!

I knew you'd want to hear this.

Mr. Frogfoot, my name is Isabel and I've been given a very important mission by the Seelie court.

We've been sent to find Miyori. We have something for him that could change the tide of the war. And you better help us, or else.

Or what?

Or the Unseelie will win.

If you could help us find Miyori, I know the Seelie would be *forever* grateful.

No.

No?!
You damp-
brained--

Enough!

What do I care
if the Seelie or
Unseelie run things?
They both try to
shut down my
business.

Give me
something of
value! Not
hot air!

You asked me to
listen and I have. But
all you have given me
are obligations to
a *losing* side.

Give me
something I
can...

No disrespect intended, sir. But the necklace is unavailable.

It's part of my mission. It's already promised to someone else.

We're not here to barter, Mr. Frogfoot, and I don't think you really see the Seelie and Unseelie as the same thing.

I hope not; I know the Unseelie hurt people in ways I pray the Seelie never did.

How long until they decide to hurt you, too?

--here!

huff, huff

Benjie? Button?

<Who are you? What are you doing in my house?>*

Huh?

*Translated from Cantonese

<GET OUT!>

I'm sorry! I--

<Thief! That little hoodlum tried to rob me!>

Slow down! You're going to hurt someone!

Where am I? Was that Clay Street?

What's that near?

She made it. Attagirl.

Your concern is touching.

Well, I don't favor brutality myself. I'm sure you're both eager to cooperate--

What do you think? Should we just ask them where their friends disappeared to?

I say we punch the answers out of them.

We're not going to tell you a root-twisted thing!

Because we don't know anything.

Really? You're just respectable businessfairies, too?

Of course not, we're thieves.

Button and I've been working together for a while. We saw the girl on the train...

...and the necklace.

And you knew its value?

I knew it was shiny and she was little.

We brought her here to fleece her.

The mushroom told her to run.

He's a little greedy. Didn't want to split it. But we want cash, not trouble.

Very well.

Spine! They're lying!

How do you know?

I saw the fungi with the girl...I think... I'm *almost* positive.

Probably true, but hardly enough. I will not have it said that the Unseelie are unjust.

Return to the palace. Perhaps the prince's oracles will be able to find this girl.

113

Didn't you hear what I was saying?

You said you'd hurt Isabel and burn down my house.

I said I remember people who helped me.

I had to make them *think* I was with them to free you.

I'm not a very big fairy, or a strong one, or a fast one.

But I told Isabel I'd get her and that necklace to Miyori. Do you remember that?

Yeah. So let's do it together.

How do I know I can trust you?

That's not how trust works, Button.

You either trust me or you don't. So, what do you say?

Why torture people for information you can't rely on, when just following them leads to so much better results?

Brilliant, ma'am.

But what if they go to the other side of the Veil? We can't follow there.

"Neither can the mushroom spirit.

"Even if the human leaves.

"They'll have to come back.

"See?"

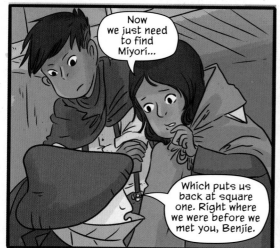

Now we just need to find Miyori...

Which puts us back at square one. Right where we were before we met you, Benjie.

But I got you a clue. Give me your map, Isabel.

Frogfoot said the warehouse was somewhere near Delancey. I know that area. It's full of warehouses; it should be dead at night.

We just have to find whatever warehouse isn't.

Have you seen any bars here? Any liquor stores?

No.

Not a lot of customers to keep that pawn shop busy right now, either.

Let's figure out why he's watching it so closely.

Yes, my lady?

What news from the front, Miyori?

Wait...

...he's Miyori?

It is unsettling. Prince Coscar's forces gain strength and may attack the city any day now.

I fear we may not be able to hold the city.

Have faith.

This...is someone's memory.

Faith? If I may speak plainly. I fear for your safety, dear heart.

We have to get you out of here before it's too late.

You're Miyori! You were there!

Where? Have you been watching me?!

"I was Princess Id'naress' personal guard for many years.

She was the bravest fairy I ever knew. I was the head of the family guard for the Seelie court.

"You may not know this, human. But Id'naress didn't just rule this city. She *was* the city.

"It was a part of her and she of it. It bent to her will.

If King Ro'hish sent it back to the city, he must have known its connection.

Holding it would have been the last time he ever held his child.

Is Id'naress... dead?

No. The necklace draws from her power, which means she must still have power to draw from.

And Ro'hish would never have sent it this close to Coscar's grasp if Id'naress wasn't just as near.

But I've searched *everywhere!*

My thanks for leading me here, human, but Frogfoot won't be getting that necklace...

...Prince Coscar will.

Benjie--?

Stay behind me, Isabel. No Unseelie is going to touch you.

The war's already over, Miyori. Your king is dead. His fortress is ours.

Just give us the necklace and we can finally bury this conflict.

Never!

144

Isabel, I'm sorry.

Frogfoot wanted the necklace and...I can't hide from him forever. I--

I know how to be a thief.

I don't want to be one but maybe I'm just a bad kid. Maybe that's why the quake took my mom and dad.

Benjie...

Don't ever think that.

You're not the only one that grownups think they can push around.

With those clothes? Your parents musta loved you.

Maybe, but Mother never said it.

"Shoulders back, legs straight. Children should be seen and not heard, Isabel."

But she was *there*.

"That was the problem. She was *just there*. And she wanted me to be *just there*, too.

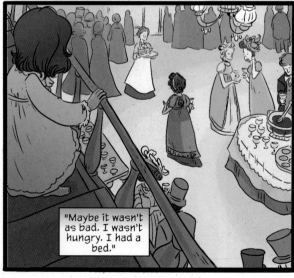

"Maybe it wasn't as bad. I wasn't hungry. I had a bed."

Isabel?

Mary!

Take care of her, please. We talked about this.

"But I always felt...in the way."

Sweetheart, you know better than to interrupt. Did you have a bad dream?

...I just wanted to say good night.

"Even Papa doesn't want me, not really."

No one thinks I can *do anything*. No one *cares* as long as I don't mess up my dress.

And no one cares what *you* want to do, either, as long as you give them what they want.

But *they're* wrong, not *us*. We're not worthless or useless.

Id'naress saw that, Benjie. She saved you.

Now she needs someone to save her!

Don't you at least want to try?

Um, Isabel?
How are we gonna
find her?

...

Miyori looked for Id'naress for months and didn't find anything.

Whole armies have looked for her. Even Frogfoot sent people out once.

How are we gonna find her when the entire fairy world can't?

I've been thinking about that.

You're right; the fairies have looked everywhere they can. But there isn't just one world, there's two because of the Veil.

You and I can move across it thanks to Id'naress' magic.

And Coscar is just as strong; he's her counterpart.

Exactly!

So what if he hid her where no other fairy could look?

This side of the Veil!

Isabel! You're a genius!

We just have to figure out where she is in this version of the city and free her!

It's still a pretty big place. I don't even know what Id'naress looks like.

She looked like...like part of the city come to life.

She had blue-gray skin, like fog. Long, pointed ears. Her hair was like wires and she wore a crown shaped like a bunch of--

--waves.

Yeah, how did you know?

Because I've seen her before, Benjie!

There was a picture of her in the newspaper...I put it in my map and I-- I don't have my map!

It must have fallen out in the fight!

It's okay. Was the newspaper recent?

Yes. But I don't have any money.

I know a place.

CLLNG!

I'VE GOT IT!

Isabel, keep it down!

Hey! You kids get outta there!

Benjie?

Oh, great. Now we've gotta run.

You can't just steal what you don't wanna pay for.

Relax! It's literally old news!

Do you think he's following us?

Nah. He can't exactly get too far from his stand or someone might steal his *actual* merchandise, not his trash.

So, what did you find?

An ad for a new art exhibit at the de Young Museum. See who's there?

That's her. It's Id'naress!

I knew it! The museum's in Golden Gate Park. It's just west of here. Follow me!

161

"...this is Coscar's palace."

"We can't break in
on the other side.
No way."

Well, then we'll just have to break in **on *this side*** of the Veil.

Have you ever broken into a place before?

Benjie, everything in my house is locked all the time.

Just help me up.

There's no window, Isabel.

Isabel... whatever you're gonna do--hurry!

Open... please?

Thank you.

169

...he fought valiantly, but in vain. And for a trinket.

It's more than a--

Wait...do you sense that?

The necklace... it's close.

Find it!

Scour the palace!

I don't get it; how was Coscar able to keep Id'naress imprisoned for so long if they're equally strong?

Fairies hate metal, especially cold iron. They can't even touch it without being hurt.

If Coscar imprisoned Id'naress in cold iron, she'd never escape.

But if fairies can't touch cold iron, how can Id'naress be inside it and still be alive?

Painfully. Very painfully.

NO!

Ah!

Urgh.

Isabel!

You defile my castle, my realm, with your very presence. You defy my will at every turn.

This is not your war, human. This is not your world.

Return my necklace and I'll return you to your side of the Veil.

Let no one say Coscar is without mercy.

You didn't show *any* mercy to Id'naress. You imprisoned her in a way that would make her suffer.

You stole her heart and hid it.

You are not a fairy! You know nothing of the plight of the Unseelie.

I know Id'naress cared about this city. She helped us when she didn't have to.

176

180

You've just lost your war.

NO!!

Your prince is defeated. Your war against us is lost. If you would fight me, do it now and you can join him.

Id'naress, don't blame them for your imprisonment. Coscar said you ran. We didn't know you were here.

Blame me. I was his captain.

Whatever punishment you choose, I will *not* run from my fate.

Your life is not what I desire, Unseelie.

This war was not my desire, either. I only wanted peace.

I cannot do that without you.

There cannot be Seelie without Unseelie, and I cannot be without a counterpart.

You must choose a new leader.

I hope you pick someone who will heal our wounds.

But it is your choice.

Spine.

It should be Spine. She's led us and she offered her life for ours.

Spine! Spine! Spine! Spine! Spine!

194

For we are one as all things are.

Seelie and Unseelie together.

Coscar was wrong to wage this war, for no balance can be achieved in extermination.

But I will also not abandon my people to a quiet destruction.

Nor would I see them go. Let this war prove only that we must stand together, or *both* be destroyed.

Though without both of you, *I* would have been destroyed.

Id'naress, Benjie is--

Do not fear, Isabel. He is easily healed.

Uhh...

Uh... Thank you.

They fought well for you, Id'naress. They refused to give up. They are truly heroes.

I'm not really a hero.

Why not? Because you stumbled from the righteous path?

I was there, Benjie. I felt everything that happened while my heart was taken from me.

And I remember the little boy I pulled from the rubble. I will not leave him again.

I name you a ward of the Seelie. Our world will not survive without insight into Humanity. If you will give us that, I will shelter you for all of your days.

You have my thanks and my love.

Thank you.

And so was the end of the last Cold Iron War.

Button! Are you alright?

You shoulda seen me, kiddo. I gave those curs what-for!

Spine reunited Button with Isabel.

Id'naress escorted them both home in the lap of luxury.

Not realizing that home was the last place Isabel wanted to go.

He wasn't interested in me when I was there.

And you did not rush to see *him* when you came back. Do you not love your father?

No! I mean, I *do*. I--I'm just scared.

Perhaps your father kept his distance because he is scared, too.

You have fought so bravely to find your voice, Isabel. Wouldn't you like your father to hear it?

I'm sorry, I--

I didn't think you would notice.

Princesa... *I'm* sorry.

I know how to work stone, and it was easier to do what I know than what I don't.

But stone cannot replace a daughter.

The rest of the summer proved him right.

It wasn't easy.

But what they made, they made together.

And by working together, even their stumbles weren't so bad.

And when the summer ended, it was hard for Isabel to leave.

Fortunately, this time she didn't have to.

Not really.

I'll visit this weekend. Okay? Be good for your mother.

I will.

Miss Isabel. I'm terribly sorry, your mother is delayed and--

No problem! Good-bye, Papa!

Now, instead of having no home, she had two.

I'll be in my room!

We're here! We're home!

One in the country...

The End

I hope you enjoyed *The City on the Other Side.*

Actually, I'm *sure* you did.

I'm so sure, in fact, that I've made a little treat for those of you who want to learn more about this book and the world inside it.

Button KNOWS EVERYTHING

Ta-da!

A lot of research went into making this book.

There actually was a terrible earthquake in San Francisco in the year 1906. It was so big it was felt from Los Angeles to Oregon!

Large portions of the city were leveled, both by the quake itself and the fires that came afterward.

The city took years to rebuild, and once they finished in 1915, they threw a party you might also have heard of: the Panama-Pacific International Exposition.

Or *San Francisco's World's Fair.*

Our book is set some time between the fire and the fair.

We don't say exactly when, though. Even fairies don't like to admit their age.

SAN FRANCISCO WORLD'S FAIR
~ 1915 ~

San Francisco is a city with a rich and diverse history.

There have been people living in this region since 3000 BCE.

San Francisco has been claimed by many.

The Spaniards took it from the Ohlone people. Then it passed to Mexico, and was finally taken by the United States.

When the Gold Rush hit in the 1840s, the city grew from a small settlement to a large metropolis.

It also became a major port for trade with Asia.

Many families like Benjie's came from China, the Philippines, and other countries to live here.

So it's always been a diverse city.

And our story reflects that in our fairies as well as our humans.

Isabel's Disguise
OR Why Mairghead doesn't draw
her own books

ISABEL

BENJIE

SPINE

Thanks to Jason, my everything.

—M.S.

Thanks to Steph and Elle for being my gracious guides to
The City and its history, to CJ and ALK for keeping me sane
through deadlines, my parents for the childhood visiting artists
in the Bay Area, and NHR, who knows what he did.

—R.R.

MAIRGHREAD SCOTT is an animation and comic book writer specializing in action-comedy. Her animation work spans such titles as *Guardians of the Galaxy*, *Ultimate Spider-Man*, *Transformers: Robots in Disguise*, and more. You can also read her work in comic book series such as: *Marvel Universe Guardians of the Galaxy*, *Transformers: Till All Are One*, *Wonder Woman 75th Anniversary Special*, and her creator-owned work *Toil and Trouble*. She is the author of the graphic novel *Science Comics: Robots & Drones*, also from First Second.

ROBIN ROBINSON draws books for both kids and adults, and has always identified with the ghosts and fairies and monsters in stories. With a background in game art as well as picture book illustration and a lifelong love of comics and animation, she has found a way to artistically nerd out in all her favorite media. Robin tries to live every day like it's Halloween.

First Second

Published by First Second
First Second is an imprint of Roaring Brook Press,
a division of Holtzbrinck Publishing Holdings Limited Partnership
175 Fifth Avenue, New York, NY 10010

Library of Congress Control Number: 2017941171

FIRST

EDITION

Hardcover ISBN: 978-1-250-15255-8
Paperback ISBN: 978-1-62672-457-0

Our books may be purchased in bulk for promotional, educational, or business use.
Please contact your local bookseller or the Macmillan Corporate and Premium Sales Department
at (800) 221-7945 ext. 5442 or by e-mail at MacmillanSpecialMarkets@macmillan.com.

First edition, 2018
Book design by Andrew Arnold, Eileen Gilshian, and Rob Steen
Lettering by Warren Montgomery
Printed in China by1010 Printing International Limited, North Point, Hong Kong

Penciled in Photoshop, inked with Frenden's "The Natural" brush in Manga Studio,
and colored in Photoshop with Robin Robinson's own brushes and textures.

1   3   5   7   9   10   8   6   4   2